Agatha
Girl of Mystery

CC

GROSSET & DUNLAP
Published by the Penguin Group
Penguin Group (USA) LLC, 375 Hudson Street, New York, New York 10014, USA

USA | Canada | UK | Ireland | Australia | New Zealand | India | South Africa | China

penguin.com
A Penguin Random House Company

Original Title: Agatha Mistery: Omicidio sulla Tour Eiffel
Text by Sir Steve Stevenson
Original cover and illustrations by Stefano Turconi

English language edition copyright © 2014 Penguin Group (USA) LLC. Original edition published by Istituto Geografico De Agostini S.p.A., Italy, © 2011 Atlantyca Dreamfarm s.r.l., Italy
International Rights © Atlantyca S.p.A.—via Leopardi 8, 20123 Milano, Italia
foreignrights@atlantyca.it—www.atlantyca.com

Published in 2014 by Grosset & Dunlap, a division of Penguin Young Readers Group, 345 Hudson Street, New York, New York 10014. GROSSET & DUNLAP is a trademark of Penguin Group (USA) LLC. Printed in the USA.

Library of Congress Cataloging-in-Publication Data is available.

10 9 8 7 6 5 4 3 2 1

ISBN 978-0-448-46223-3

Agatha

Girl of Mystery

The Eiffel Tower Incident

by Sir Steve Stevenson
illustrated by Stefano Turconi

translated by Siobhan Tracey
adapted by Maya Gold

Grosset & Dunlap
An Imprint of Penguin Group (USA) LLC

FIFTH MISSION
Agents

Agatha
Twelve years old, an
aspiring mystery writer;
has a formidable memory

Dash
Agatha's cousin and student
at the private school Eye
International Detective Academy

Chandler
Butler and former boxer with impeccable British style

Watson
Obnoxious Siberian cat with the nose of a bloodhound

Gaston
A bohemian painter living in a Paris attic

DESTINATION

Paris, France

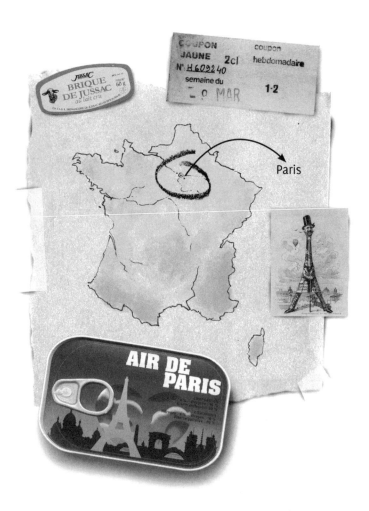

Paris

OBJECTIVE

Track down the murderer of Russian diplomat Boris Renko, who was poisoned at one of the world's most famous monuments: the Eiffel Tower!

Dedicated to Frida, who is with me through all my stories, both real and fictional

Thanks to the hundreds of people, young and old, who have supported not just Agatha and Dash's adventures, but all children's detective stories. A special thanks to Monia Grisendi and Stefania Erlino (BiblioDays di Novellara), Emanuele Vietina (Lucca Comics and Games), and Ilaria Avanzi (Noir in Festival di Courmayeur). Without their help, none of this would have been possible.

The Investigation Begins...

Waking up at eight in the morning was not at the top of Dashiell Mistery's wish list. To keep from falling asleep on camera during a videoconference on Decoding, his last class before the holiday break, the Eye International student detective drank can after can of Coke. It gurgled and fizzed in his belly.

But it wasn't just the snooze-inducing lesson that made him squirm. Out of the window of his mother's penthouse apartment, he could see a huge mass of dark clouds rolling toward central London. A blizzard was on the way. Dash peered at the thermometer outside the window

and let out a gasp. "No way . . . it's dropped five degrees!"

It was sure to start snowing any minute.

Dash grabbed his laptop to check the weather websites. Their headlines read "The Storm of the Year" and "One of the City's Top Ten."

"Ugh," Dash grumbled. "I've been looking forward to a sweet vacation in Paris with my brother, Gaston. If I don't make my move right away, I'll be stuck at home until the storm is over."

Keeping his eyes fixed on the webcam so none of the other videoconference participants would suspect anything, Dash slowly moved his fingers over the keyboard.

"Let's roll out a few technical difficulties," he mumbled, running a hand through his mop of black hair.

He casually clicked the settings menu and launched a program named *Electronic Tsunami*.

Almost instantaneously, a slight waviness appeared on-screen, followed by a flickering that distorted and fuzzed out his image.

Within moments, the screen looked as though it had been inundated by a devastating tidal wave of static and distortion. The finicky Decoding professor noticed it first, interrupting her lesson. "What's going on, Agent DM14?" she asked, irritated. Then her tone got more urgent. "Agent DM14? Are you still connected?"

Dash began to simulate audio distortion, twisting the foam microphone cover between his fingers. "I'm . . . *FRUSHHHHH* . . . losing . . . *FRUSHHHHH* . . . the signal!" he said, doing his best to sound concerned. "It must be because of the . . . *FRUSHHHH* . . . storm!"

Seconds later, the whole screen went black. He quickly shut down his computer and took off his earbuds. "I'm the man, Dash!" he cried, pumping his fists in a victory dance. "No one

can fool them like Dash can!"

He gulped down the last of his Coke and tossed the can on top of the teetering pile of trash on his desk. After pulling on his winter coat, hat, and gloves, he paused in front of an unusual cell phone hooked up to its charger.

It was his EyeNet, a valuable high-tech gadget given to him by his detective school.

The sleek device was a treasure trove of technological innovations that enabled the students of Eye International to carry out their investigative missions all around the world.

He stood for a moment, one hand on his EyeNet. He rarely let it out of his sight, but he was heading off on a family vacation and didn't want to think about school until after New Year's Day. After a moment, he made up his mind. "You'll be safe here . . . I wouldn't want to drop you from the top of the Eiffel Tower!"

He left the EyeNet back on its charger, grabbed

his bags, and closed the door, locking it with three different keys. His mother's apartment was not far from St. Pancras railway station, where he would board the "Chunnel train"—the Eurostar that ran through a tunnel under the English Channel. It could reach speeds of more than a hundred and eighty miles an hour, and it would take just two and a half hours to reach the French capital. It was the kind of technological advance that sent shivers of excitement up Dash's spine.

"I'll get to Gaston's in time for lunch," he said as he walked across the street, ignoring the first white flakes dancing through the air. "It's so much better than having to take a plane!"

His thoughts drifted to his beloved cousin Agatha, who had left for Paris at dawn along with her butler, Chandler, and Watson the cat. They were probably already sitting in Gaston's studio in Paris with Agatha boring them all silly, rambling about French culture and art.

Lost in thought, Dash arrived at St. Pancras in plenty of time. The next train for Paris was leaving in half an hour. As he entered the railway station, he stared at the huge metal arches, the mirrored walkways, and the sleek high-speed trains sitting on the tracks. It looked like a futuristic spaceport.

"Wow!" he exclaimed, excited.

A voice from behind froze him in his tracks. "Agent DM14? What are you doing here?" Dash didn't have to turn around to know who that squeaky voice belonged to. It was his Practical Investigations professor, code name UM60.

What was the professor doing at St. Pancras station? Had he come to punish Dash for his hasty escape from Decoding class?

Flushing red with embarrassment, Dash began to stammer an apology. "Uh, oh, so sorry about the videoconference. I promise it won't ever happen again!"

"I don't know what you're talking about,

detective," Agent UM60 replied dryly. "And I don't really care. I have far more important things on my mind!"

The boy let out a sigh of relief. For the first time, he gathered the courage to turn and face his professor. He had to lower his gaze significantly, since Agent UM60 was about half his height.

Since he was used to seeing his professor on a computer screen, Dash had never realized how much the little man looked like a penguin with a bowler hat on his head. He had to stifle a laugh.

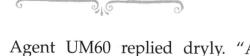

"Something wrong, Agent DM14?" the professor asked, bristling.

"Uh, no . . . hee-hee . . . I swear."

"Why are you staring at me like that?"

"I see you've got your briefcase

with you . . . are you going somewhere?" asked Dash, doing his best to distract him.

"I should think that is obvious," Agent UM60 sniffed. "I'm taking the next train to Paris. I've got a very important case to solve, detective." He reached up to smooth his waxed mustache.

Dash could hardly contain his laughter. To cover it, he grabbed the professor's briefcase. He barely had time to blurt, "Let me help you with that," before he took off like a rocket across the platform.

Unfortunately, he hadn't noticed the strong chain from the briefcase to his teacher's wrist.

And so, with a violent jerk and a scream of pain, detective Dashiell Mistery began one of the longest days of his life—and the most dangerous case of his young career.

Gaston's Studio

*T*welve-year-old Agatha had known for a long time that every member of the Mistery family was a little eccentric. She recalled Christmas dinners at her grandparents' mansion, the long table heaped high with exotic foods, surrounded by chattering aunts and uncles, cousins and distant relatives. Her family was spread out all over the world, and since every Mistery had an unusual job and spoke the language of whatever country in which they lived, family gatherings always turned into lively, international affairs that the United Nations would have envied.

The most eccentric of all was Dash's father,

Edgar Allan Mistery. He was constantly changing professions as he pursued his countless and varied passions. He had taught himself so many languages that he was no longer able to count them. Above all, he married and divorced with great carelessness. His most recent marriage, to a Norwegian speed-skating champion, had produced a little blond girl named Ilse. Dash was the middle child, born in London while Edgar was working as a landscape designer to Her Royal Highness, the Queen of England. His eldest son, Gaston, had been born in Paris, when Edgar was a celebrity dog groomer in the *Ville Lumière.*

Gaston was now twenty years old, an art student at the prestigious Academie Belle Époque. He spent most of his days in an attic studio overlooking the churchyard of Notre Dame. Gaston was tall and thin, with an explosion of curly hair and a jacket perpetually smeared with different colored paints.

"Don't touch your nose, cousin," Gaston told Agatha. She was perched on an armchair that had been angled against the window to catch the north light. "Stay just like that a bit longer. I want to capture all of your wit, *ma cherie!*"

Agatha suppressed a smile. It was typical of Gaston to scatter his sentences with French exclamations and terms of endearment. But she wasn't feeling especially witty at the moment, since she was chilled to the bone. An arctic wind rattled the windows, and the woodstove in Gaston's living room couldn't compete.

Watson, her fluffy Siberian cat, had found himself a cozy spot right in front of the fire.

"So you really want to be a writer?" asked

Gaston after a moment. He stepped back from his easel, clutching a stub of charcoal between his long fingers.

"It's all right to speak now?"

"*Oui*, but of course!" her cousin excused himself. "Your sketch is finished!"

Agatha jumped to her feet, rubbing her hands together to bring back the circulation. "I adore writing," she said, adding shyly, "But I still have a lot to learn!"

"What sort of books do you prefer?"

"Mystery stories, full of twists and turns . . ."

"You mean detective novels?"

Agatha burst out laughing. "Yes, especially stories with bumbling detectives who can't find

the culprit without an unexpected stroke of luck," she said, smiling at the thought of her hapless cousin Dash, who had been her companion through innumerable adventures.

It was almost noon, and he would be arriving any minute. Knowing Dash, he'd spend the whole day complaining about the snowstorm.

"When was the last time you saw your brother?" she asked Gaston.

Gaston turned to look for something, digging among the piles of paintings and sketches stacked everywhere. He stopped to stroke his bohemian sideburns, then reached into a pile and pulled out a dusty frame. "Here it is!" he exclaimed with satisfaction, dusting it off with one sleeve. "The last time he came to visit, Dash looked like a plucked chicken!"

He handed the picture to Agatha, who let out a giggle. Her cousin had a buzz cut, chubby cheeks, and a sulky expression. With a touch of

irony, Gaston had drawn him with chicken feet instead of shoes.

"What a grouch he was as a ten-year-old," she commented cheerfully. "Not much has changed!"

Gaston looked at the picture, stunned. "How did you know he was ten years old?"

Agatha shrugged. "The date is written right here at the bottom."

"*Mais oui*, how silly of me!" Gaston laughed. Then he winked, adding, "I've heard that you don't miss a thing, *ma petite* Agatha!"

Just then, Watson's ears pricked up at the sound of heavy footsteps in the bedroom. When the door creaked open to reveal Chandler's imposing profile, the cat put his head down and went back to sleep.

"May I please keep the robe on?" Chandler asked politely. "I don't want to catch a nasty cold . . ."

The young artist spun around happily. "I've

never painted a boxer so strong and muscular," he exclaimed with delight. "It will be *extraordinaire*!"

"Do you really think so, Master Gaston?" asked Chandler, dubiously contemplating the red boxing gloves he had been asked to wear for the group portrait.

Agatha came to his rescue. "It won't take him long," she said, turning to her cousin. "Isn't that right?"

"*Oui*, just a few minutes," the painter confirmed. "A quick life drawing."

Chandler hunched forward, crossing the room. He positioned himself next to the armchair and reluctantly removed the robe so he was posing in just his boxing shorts.

"Now raise your fists, puff out your chest, and look tough," Gaston coached him.

The big man obeyed without complaint. In his role as jack-of-all-trades for Agatha and her parents, he was used to finding himself in all kinds

of bizarre situations.

An eerie silence fell over the studio as Gaston went to work. The young girl leaned against the windowsill, staring out at the rooftops of Paris. Christmas lights twinkled everywhere, and people walked fast on the sidewalks below, hunching their shoulders against the harsh wind. Beyond, she could see Notre Dame, resplendent in its Gothic glory. The sight filled her imagination with scenes for a novel set in Paris during the cathedral's

construction. The plot would be full of crimes and conspiracies.

Struck by inspiration, Agatha pulled her trusty notebook out of her bag to jot down some notes. She would have liked to consult a history book, but there was nothing in Gaston's studio but canvases, tubes of paint, brushes, and other painting paraphernalia.

She picked up her favorite pen and began to write with the utmost concentration.

Everyone was so immersed in his or her work that it took them a while to notice an insistent knocking at the door.

"Let me in, I'm frozen solid!" shouted Dash Mistery, in tones of despair.

Gaston rushed to the door, unlocked it, and greeted his brother with a warm hug.

But Dash was his usual self. "I've been ringing your doorbell for the past half hour!" His whining could be heard all the way to the living

room. "Are you all deaf?"

"*Pardon*, the bell is broken!" replied Gaston, leading him into the room.

"The elevator, too?"

"Six flights of stairs is hardly a formidable workout!"

As Dash shook the snow off his jacket, he caught sight of Chandler, dressed like a boxer ready to step into the ring.

"Hey!" he cried. "Are you crazy? It's freezing, and you're wearing *shorts*?"

Agatha shot back, "What about you? Why are you wearing sunglasses on such a dark day?"

The young detective had peeled off his snow-covered jacket, gloves, and hat, but he was still wearing a pair of dark glasses with light-emitting diodes, or LEDs, on the frames.

"Um, oh, these old things?" he mumbled. "Patience, cousin, I can't explain everything right this minute . . ." He pursed his lips, handing

her a copy of the daily paper, *Le Figaro,* with a significant look.

"I'm painting a family portrait," Gaston explained. "Are you ready to pose?"

"May I get dressed now?" asked Chandler, still frozen in a fighting stance.

"Oui, Monsieur Chandler!"

The faithful servant touched his jaw with an enormous red glove, then disappeared into the bathroom to put on his spotless tuxedo. In the meantime, Dash was dragged by one arm to stand in front of the easel.

"You see?" Gaston urged him. "I've already sketched Watson, Agatha, and Chandler. Now it's your turn to pose!"

"Um... I just got off the train, in a snowstorm... I wouldn't mind having a hamburger first," Dash replied. "Couldn't you just paint me from memory?"

Gaston glared at him with wounded artistic

pride. "Memory? But you've changed so much since the last time I saw you, Dash! You've become . . . a young man!"

"Here, this photo might help," said Agatha. She glanced at the headline of the newspaper before stashing it inside her bag, then handed Gaston a recent photo of herself and Dash in the Mistery House gardens, adding, "Trust me, you don't want to be around Dash when he's hungry. And while you're at work on your painting, we'll go see the sights. I can't wait to visit the Eiffel Tower!"

Dash nodded, his expression indecipherable behind his dark glasses.

Agatha called Chandler, and they all got wrapped up in winter layers. Dash kept grumbling that his coat hadn't even dried off yet.

As the three Londoners got ready to leave, Gaston stopped them with a request. "I've run

out of cobalt blue. Do you think you could pick up another tube for me?"

"You can count on us," Agatha promised, her eyes sparkling. "We're on the case." The newspaper's headline had given her a fresh jolt of energy.

The Restaurant in the Sky

The threesome hurried along the icy sidewalk to the Saint-Germain-des-Prés Metro station. The wind whipped through the bare trees, and they turned up the collars of their warm jackets as the snow whirled all around them.

It was definitely not the ideal day to admire the beauty of Paris.

Watson poked his nose out of his carrying case, which Chandler was toting. He sniffed at the cold air, then immediately curled up inside where it was warm.

Agatha led them into a traditional bistro, brightly lit and full of people. As soon as they sat down at one of the tables, she pulled the newspaper out of her bag, jabbing her finger at the front page. "A murder, Dash?" she asked bluntly. "What sort of mess have you gotten yourself into this time?"

Startled, Chandler bolted upright in his chair and nearly knocked over a set of glasses.

"I know, I know . . . I've ruined our winter vacation," the young detective mumbled in distress. "But I promise

I can explain everything!"

Agatha smiled at him. "No worries about the vacation, dear cousin," she reassured him. "But why has Eye International entrusted you with investigating such a serious crime? No offense, but you're still a rookie."

She had a good point. Dash's special assignments were usually limited to theft, fraud, and kidnapping, while homicide cases were given to Eye International's most expert detectives.

He looked around warily, then leaned across the table. "You want to know the truth?" he asked in a barely audible whisper.

Agatha and Chandler nodded decisively, inviting him to explain.

"I'm working on behalf of Agent UM60," the boy revealed. "He injured his leg while waiting for the Eurostar, and I was the only agent within range that he could entrust with the top-secret documents pertaining to the case. It's an

extraordinary coincidence, don't you think?"

Dash failed to mention that the accident was the result of his own carelessness, and that the professor was in the hospital with his broken leg in traction. He instantly regretted this omission; Agatha had a talent for intuiting any sort of lie. To verify his story, he pulled a small, square device out of his pocket. "This is the EyeNet Plus that Agent UM60 lent me for the mission," he boasted. "It's a much more advanced model than mine."

"What about those geeky glasses with the flashing lights?" asked his cousin.

"They have special multifunctional lenses used to collect information at crime scenes," Dash said proudly. "The professor told me never to take them off, not even when I go to sleep!" He punctuated this last sentence with a nervous laugh. He had noticed that Agatha was stroking her small, upturned nose, as she always did

when she had one of her incredible flashes of inspiration.

Luckily for Dash, the waitress arrived to take their order on her notepad.

"Do you have any preferences?" asked Agatha, the only one in the group who spoke French. "If not, I suggest a traditional Parisian lunch."

They had no objections, so Agatha ordered an *"assortiment de fromages"* and returned her attention to the investigation.

"All right, my dear colleagues," she began. "The details in the newspaper are very intriguing. I can summarize them in three short points. Are you ready?"

The others were all ears.

"First point: the victim is Boris Renko, a sixty-year-old Russian diplomat who was working at the embassy in Paris."

Dash punched the name into his device,

instantly scanning Eye International's vast database.

"Found him!" he exclaimed, beaming. "Go on, cousin!"

"Second point: the crime took place in the famous Jules Verne restaurant, on the second level of the Eiffel Tower, more than four hundred feet above the ground. Unfortunately, the French police have cordoned off the whole area, and the restaurant will remain closed while they investigate."

"Which means, alas, that we can say good-bye to tracking down any clues at the scene of the crime," said Chandler. "They won't let us near it."

Agatha regretfully agreed. "Hopefully, Dash can access lots of information about the Jules Verne on his EyeNet Plus. Otherwise we're doomed."

Dash wasted no time. "I've got detailed

blueprints, a complete list of staff members, and the names of the hundred and twenty guests who had reservations last night," he said enthusiastically. "My professor already started a search!"

"Excellent," said Agatha happily. "Bookmark it all now. We can access his files when we need further details."

"What is the third point, Miss Agatha?" the butler prompted.

"Let's have a taste of this first," replied his young mistress, hungrily eyeing the large cheese board the waitress had just set down in the middle of their table. The service had been very fast, maybe because the bistro was full of tourists

seeking refuge from the cold and the whole staff was working.

Dash sniffed suspiciously. "What is that smell?" he asked with a grimace. "I think something's gone bad."

"French cheeses are some of the world's most unique," Agatha explained as she smeared some soft Brie on a slice of crusty baguette. "Taste them, Dash, they're exquisite!"

He cut off a small corner of Camembert, a specialty from Normandy with a crusty white rind, and started to chew. A moment later, his face turned green. "This cheese is moldy!" he squealed in disgust. "Do they all taste like stinky socks?"

"A bit of mold just adds to the flavor; isn't that right, Chandler?" Agatha teased.

The butler was devouring a big slice of Roquefort, a particularly odorous sheep cheese striped with veins of blue mold. "It's delicious, Miss Agatha," he agreed.

"If you like your cheese rotten," Dash grumbled, crossing his arms. His stomach growled loudly, but he sat through the whole meal without touching another bite. "Where were we?" he snapped when the waitress took the empty cheese board away.

Agatha wiped her mouth with a napkin and checked the newspaper. "Right here," she said, dropping her voice. "The thing that bothers me most is the way that Boris Renko was murdered."

"The newspaper says he was poisoned, right?"

"That's right, Dash, but the police determined the cause of death a few hours after it happened!"

"I don't get it."

Agatha pushed back her hair and began to think. After a moment, she clasped her hands together and said, "Let's try to reconstruct the facts." She held up the press photo on the front page, which showed a man sprawled on the floor between the elegant tables at the Jules Verne.

"This was taken at nine fifteen p.m., when Mr. Renko, who was dining alone, suddenly fainted. At first, the restaurant's owners thought he was simply unwell and called an ambulance. However, at about eleven thirty p.m., he was pronounced dead at the hospital. The police discovered traces of poison in his wine and immediately arrested the sommelier who had been serving him."

"So they've already caught the culprit?" Dash's voice was hopeful. He was always in a hurry to wrap up an investigation. "Case closed!"

"The fingerprints on the wineglass do implicate the sommelier," Agatha said. "But I have the distinct feeling he's innocent. It would have been pretty stupid on his part to leave such an obvious clue . . . and he had to touch the glass when he set it down in front of his customer," she mused, tapping her nose with one finger. "I propose a different scenario . . ."

"What?" Dash and Chandler asked in chorus.

She bit her bottom lip and explained. "It's far more likely the assassin was one of the guests at the restaurant. He or she could have slipped the lethal substance into Mr. Renko's glass, then calmly walked out of the restaurant. No one even realized it was a homicide until eleven thirty p.m.!"

Agatha's version seemed plausible, but there was still one big problem.

"How are we going to interview more than a hundred suspects, Miss?" Chandler asked, sounding worried.

Dash put his face in his hands. "Just tracking all of them down will take ages," he groaned. "And some of them probably left Paris before the storm hit!"

Agatha pointed at the EyeNet Plus on the table. "Didn't you say your professor had already started to work on the case?" she suggested. "Check and see if there's anything useful."

He grabbed the device and frantically began to type. "Uh-oh . . . so many passwords . . . the security's very complex," he muttered. "I can't access the main menu . . . Wait, no, here it is. Got it!"

A moment later, Dash raised his head, beaming. "My dear colleagues, we've hit the jackpot," he announced solemnly. "This audio file should lead us straight to the culprit!"

The Search Goes Underground

*T*he three investigators took turns using the EyeNet's earbuds to replay the recording of Boris Renko's last, brief phone call: a distress call made to Eye International at 9:15 p.m. on the previous evening.

Dash listened first. He looked disappointed.

Next came Chandler, who raised an eyebrow without saying a word.

Finally it was Agatha's turn. She listened twice, then quietly repeated the two words of Renko's recording: "Red rose."

What could it mean?

The chatter of tourists in the bistro seemed

even louder in the silence that fell over their table. Each of them tried to understand what the victim might have been trying to say with those fateful last words.

"Maybe it's a brand of wine," Dash guessed. "The poisoned wine that killed Mr. Renko!"

They quickly checked the information supplied by the EyeNet. The cellar of the Jules Verne stocked a selection of red and white wines, carefully chosen to appeal to the most refined palates. Though most of the names were in French, there was nothing to do with a red rose.

The butler put forth his own theory. "Could it be a gift he received from the murderer?" he asked. "Suppose he approached Mr. Renko's table with a rose, and used the moment of distraction to slip the poison into his wineglass."

"Impossible." Dash shook his head. "The restaurant staff would have found the rose at the scene and handed it to the police as evidence."

Agatha nodded. She was busily browsing through the pages of the newspaper.

"Got any brilliant ideas?" asked Dash hopefully. "We're just stumbling around in the dark!"

She stroked her nose. "Red rose could mean anything," she declared. "Our task is to narrow the field of possibilities."

"The restaurant's surveillance camera!" Dash cried, excited. "We'd be able to look for any red rose on the crime scene!"

Chandler cleared his throat. "I don't wish to disappoint you, Master Dash," he said politely, "but I'm sure the Paris police have impounded that video footage by now."

Once again, Agatha nodded, this time with a knowing smile indicating that something had clicked into place.

"Don't keep us in suspense," Dash protested. "Tell us what ace you've got up your sleeve!"

Agatha pulled out one of the inside pages of the newspaper, placing it next to the front page. "What do these two photos have in common?"

"The victim," said Dash. "Both show Boris Renko stretched out on the ground, but they're taken from two different angles."

"Look closer!"

"Ugh, I hate riddles," he muttered.

It was Chandler who figured out what his young mistress was after. "The same agency sold both photographs to *Le Figaro*."

"Well done, Chandler," Agatha congratulated him. "So we can assume they were both taken by the same photographer. When my mother goes to get her hair done, I always skim through the gossip magazines. If my memory serves me correctly, agencies buy photos from the paparazzi who specialize in getting the hottest scoops."

"But paparazzi go after celebrities," said Dash, skimming the list of restaurant guests.

"What was a professional photographer doing at the Jules Verne last night?"

"Let's ask him ourselves!" declared Agatha. She sprang into action, phoning the agency for the photographer's contact information. Dash ran it through a search engine and found his address. They paid for their lunch and stepped out to face the snowstorm with renewed courage.

The Metro train was packed with travelers, but Chandler shouldered his way inside. As it pulled out of the underground station, Agatha became pensive. "We need a plan," she reflected aloud. "Those photos were bought for a huge sum of money."

"Uh-oh; I've only got a handful of change in my pocket," Dash mumbled, readjusting his glasses.

Agatha turned to stare at him. "What did you say those souped-up goggles could do?" she asked.

Chandler petted Watson as they whispered among themselves.

Just before three in the afternoon, they entered a secluded back alley in Montmartre, a hilly district full of musicians and all sorts of artists. They found the photographer's name on the wrought-iron gate, and pressed the intercom button without hesitation.

"*Bonjour, monsieur,* we're from the *Times* of London, and we'd like exclusive rights to any remaining photos from the Jules Verne restaurant," said Agatha in perfect French.

"Sixth floor," croaked a hoarse voice. "Second door on the left."

As they climbed the narrow staircase, Dash panted, "Isn't there one working elevator in the whole of Paris?"

"Focus," replied his cousin. "It's imperative that we don't make any mistakes."

"Yes, ma'am," said Dash, making a mock military salute.

The apartment door stood open. It was dark inside, and the air was so thick with cigar smoke that it almost seemed to be coming out of the furniture.

"May we come in?" asked Agatha.

"I'm in the darkroom!" answered the same gravelly voice. "Don't turn on the lights!"

They stumbled through the musty foyer and felt their way down the hallway. In a small room at the very end, lit only by a red light, stood an elderly man with thinning hair and a protruding

belly. He had deep bags under his eyes and continued to develop his photos without any regard for his guests, swishing them through a stop bath with tongs.

"Sorry to break it to you, but the best photos of Renko are already sold," he warned them from a haze of cigar fumes. "I scored some big bucks on that gig!"

Agatha joined him next the trays of developing chemicals. "We'd like to see the rest anyway," she said politely. "Who knows, maybe we'll find one that hasn't been seen yet . . ."

He pointed at a pile of prints. "Good luck," he said with a croaking laugh. "I can always use some more cash!"

While Dash looked through the photos with Chandler's help, Agatha used her formidable interrogation skills to question the photographer. "Nice to see someone who hasn't gone digital yet," she flattered. "I've always preferred classic

black-and-white prints. So what brought you to the Jules Verne last night?"

"Got a tip from a source," he said, chewing his cigar butt. "He told me a famous TV star was gonna be dining out with her new flame, so I put my camera in a strategic position and activated the automatic shutter release."

"Let me guess. Your TV star never showed up."

He peered at a strip of negatives, holding it up to the red light. "You got it," he said, nodding. "If that Russian guy hadn't croaked, the whole night would've been a big bust."

"Did you see what happened?"

"I was too far away, but I heard someone shout when the Russki collapsed," the photographer rasped. "Soon as I heard it, I swiveled that way with my camera, but some security goon pulled me out of there before I got many shots. Still, it was better than nothing—the agency paid me a good chunk of change for those shots of the stiff on the rug."

Agatha couldn't stand such insensitive behavior—the poor man had died, after all. She cast an eye over at Chandler and Dash, who flashed a discreet thumbs-up.

"Thanks for your time, but we didn't find anything we can use in our newspaper."

"Told you so," he smirked. "If you ever need

celebrity photos, give me a shout. I'm the best in the biz."

"Count on it," Agatha lied, fuming. "You can totally count on it!"

They left the apartment without as much as a good-bye. On the landing, Dash flashed an encouraging smile and tapped on the rims of his glasses. "I recorded them all, one by one," he exclaimed. "As soon as I upload them onto the EyeNet, we'll be able to zoom in on details all over the restaurant!"

They ducked into a cybercafe with WiFi, where they could synch up UM60's files with the photographs. They sat in a quiet corner, checking each photo against the list of guests and the seating plan. It took more than half an hour to go through them all, but the result was even better than they could have hoped.

"We've found three people who could be called a 'red rose,'" Agatha said at long last,

satisfied with their work. "Who would you like to start with, colleagues?"

Dash picked the most suspicious "red rose" on the list, a boxer called Gerard Clouseau. "I don't trust his face," he said, looking at the photo. "In the file, it says he trains at a boxing gym in Montparnasse."

Agatha smiled. "That's on the Left Bank, all the way across town . . . What are we waiting for? Let's go track him down!"

CHAPTER FOUR
The Great Challenge

"Not another long tunnel," grumbled Dash, holding on to the triple-branched support pole as their Metro train burrowed underneath the River Seine. "As if taking a train under the English Channel wasn't bad enough . . . I'm starting to get claustrophobic!"

Short and petite, Agatha was pressed among a crowd of tourists and commuters. She craned her neck toward the window, observing the flashing lights of the mysterious Paris underground with rapt fascination. "Did you know that there's a whole other world under Paris?" she said. "I just opened one of my memory drawers and a

book my father used to read as a bedtime story popped into my mind. It's called *Les Miserables*. Parts of it are set in the vast network of sewers and catacombs under the city streets."

Even in a tight spot like this, pressed against a woolly sleeve clutching a loaf of French bread, Agatha's imagination turned toward stories. But if books were her favorite subject, the same could not be said for her cousin.

"Uh . . . cat . . . catacombs?" Dash was known for his dislike of cats, especially Watson.

"Catacombs are ancient underground tombs. Nothing to do with cats!" Agatha laughed, then looked at Chandler, who stood by her side like a bodyguard. "Let's get back to our suspect. Could you please summarize the information in his file?"

"Certainly, Miss Agatha," the butler replied promptly.

Ignoring Watson, who was stretching out a

paw from inside his carrier, Chandler gave a brief biography of Gerard Clouseau. Twenty-seven years old, originally from a tough neighborhood in the port of Marseilles, he was a bit of a bad boy with several convictions for brawling. His talent for boxing had probably saved him from a life of violent crime.

Nonetheless, as the three Londoners soon found out, he still had a temper.

As soon as he saw the small group enter the gym, the young boxer stopped trading punches with his sparring partner, leaning against the ropes with a swaggering air.

"We're private detectives, and we want you to tell us what happened last night at the Jules Verne restaurant. It's a homicide case," Agatha announced without mincing words.

"I thought I smelled cops," sneered the boxer. "And I've never liked cops, especially runt cops like you . . . Since when did the police start

recruiting kids? Why don't you brats run along and play instead of interrupting my training?" Gerard Clouseau was wiry and muscular. He had tattoos running up both arms, ending at the neck with a thorny rose. A *red rose*. He turned his back on them, strutting back into the ring. "I didn't kill anyone. End of story."

Agatha sighed, turning toward Dash and Chandler, who was petting the increasingly restless Watson.

"Just the attitude we'd expect from a man who's got something to hide," Dash whispered into her ear. "At school, they taught us to pay attention to a suspect's first statement," he added, his voice trembling. "If you ask me, he did it. He's got a red rose tattooed on his neck, a violent past, and he's hiding something for sure . . . we just have to flush him out!"

Agatha glanced around the gym. Several young men were training with jump ropes while

others pummeled punching bags with red boxing gloves.

Her face lit up and she called out to Gerard Clouseau, waving her hand. She'd thought of the perfect way to capture his interest.

"What do you want now?" roared the boxer. "You're messing up my training!"

Agatha flashed him a mischievous smile. "You call this training?" she goaded him. "How would you like to box with a real champion?"

"Who, that skinny punk with the weird sunglasses?" laughed the boxer, puffing up his sweaty chest. "Come on, get a grip. He's a wimp!"

Dash's hair stood on end. "Uh-oh . . . did I hear that right? I . . . what are you trying to do to me?" he babbled.

Just then, Chandler stood up to his full height. Handing Watson back to his young mistress, he loosened the bow tie on his tuxedo. "Leave it to me, Master Dash," he declared firmly.

An elderly attendant went to get Chandler some gloves and led him to the locker room. The butler was ready in minutes, wearing boxing gear for the second time that day. It had been years since his last professional bout in the ring.

News of the challenge spread around the gym and a crowd of onlookers gathered around the ring, ready to bet on the hometown favorite.

At the sound of the bell, Gerard Clouseau began bobbing and weaving around the butler, whose movements were solid and slow.

A pair of lightning-fast lefts caught Chandler in the side, followed by a well-aimed right hook to the head. A series of jabs and uppercuts followed, which the butler took without batting an eyelid.

"You're a dinosaur," taunted the younger boxer. "You'll never get close enough to even touch me!"

He spoke too soon. With one sudden,

devastating thrust of his arm, Chandler punched the younger boxer square on the jaw. With a single blow, Clouseau collapsed onto the mat, out cold.

Dash and Agatha, who had been holding their breath in fear that Chandler would be hurt, climbed into the ring to congratulate him. The rest of the gym burst into applause and laughter. It was the fastest bout anyone could remember.

But what now? How were they going to wake Gerard Clouseau?

The task was taken on by the elderly attendant, who dragged the tattooed boxer into the locker room and stuck his head under the cold water.

"Wh-wh-wh-what happened?" stammered the muscular young man.

"You were schooled, that's what happened," replied the attendant good-naturedly. "These people want to ask you some questions. Think you still can string a sentence together?"

"Eh? What? What happened to that ugly bulldog?" asked the boxer, confused by Agatha and her companions. "Oh, man, there he is! Ask me whatever you want, I give up!"

Agatha pulled out the Jules Verne blueprints, pointing to a table near the victim's. "Were you sitting here last night?" she asked drily.

He confirmed with a groan, pressing an ice pack against his swelling eye. "Yeah, my manager took me out for dinner. We were toasting the boxing tour I'm doing in South America," he said. "But I swear I had nothing to do with the murder of that nasty Russian!"

Agatha rested her

chin on crossed hands and asked, curious, "Why didn't you like him? How well did you know each other?"

"No . . . *ouch* . . . I never laid eyes on him before last night."

Agatha snapped her fingers, her eyes lighting up. "Of course! I've studied the guidebooks, and if memory serves me correctly, there's a private elevator that goes directly to the restaurant on the second level. You had a fight with him on the way up, am I right?"

"H-how did you know that?"

Gerard Clouseau was even more shocked than Dash and Chandler, who already knew about the girl's incredible intuition.

"You booked tables at the same time; therefore it's logical that you would have ridden up in the same elevator," said Agatha. "What was said during that four-hundred-foot ride?"

The boxer shook his head. "I wanted to punch

him out," he admitted, still angry. "That moron got up in my face about what I was wearing: sleeveless top, chains, baggy pants. He told me I looked like a rapper, that tourists were spoiling the atmosphere of the world's most elegant restaurant!" he growled. "This Russian guy has the nerve to call *me* a tourist? It was an insult, and I wanted to make him pay." He clenched his fists, groaning in pain. "But my manager held me back. That was the only time I spoke to that Renko dude."

"Just as I thought," Agatha said with a sigh. She thanked Clouseau, gingerly shaking his bandaged hand, and led the way to the door.

Dash was right on her heels, saying stubbornly, "He did it! I know he did! Why don't we grill him some more?"

Chandler interjected calmly, "That was a dead end, young sir."

"Why?" cried the student detective. "He's got

a red rose tattooed on his neck, and a fight in the elevator is an unshakable motive!"

"Dearest cousin, did he seem like the type who'd use poison to settle an argument?" asked Agatha. "He didn't even know Boris Renko. He's just a street fighter with a puffed-up ego. I hope Chandler's right hook took him down a notch."

When they got back on the Metro, Dash sprawled across two empty seats. "We're wasting so much time!" he exclaimed. "My whole detective career is at stake!"

It was almost five o'clock.

"Calm down, Dash," his cousin encouraged him. "I've just opened one of my memory drawers, and I recall that in the encyclopedia of poisons, there's a substance that produces an effect similar to fainting and is lethal after a couple of hours. Strychnine."

"Strychnine?" Dash repeated. "What is it?"

"Rat poison, Master Dash," the butler explained. "I scatter it in the Mistery House cellar once a week because Watson treats rodents like playmates."

Dash raised an eyebrow, intrigued. "You want to go to the Eiffel Tower to see if there are traces of strychnine in the restaurant?"

"Actually, I was thinking we should pay a visit to our next suspect," replied Agatha, tucking a stray lock of hair away. "Could you set your spy glasses to search for traces of strychnine?"

"Uh . . . I think so!"

Dash pulled out the EyeNet Plus and pushed a sequence of buttons, causing the LEDs on the glasses to blink. "Great! There's a 'Search Poisons' function. I'm setting it to scan for any toxic substances," he said with renewed energy. "Who are we going to see next?"

Agatha gave him a little smile. "The next

stop is the hotel Coeur Amoureux, where I hope we'll flush out our *red rose*," she replied with a wink.

CHAPTER FIVE
The Avenue of Broken Dreams

The majestic Avenue des Champs-Élysées was lined with cafés, movie theaters, and upscale boutiques. Holiday lights sparkled on manicured trees. Despite all this glamour, Parisians scurried past wrapped up in coats or under the shelter of umbrellas, their eyes never leaving the pavement.

Dash was trying to see where he was going by pushing his dark glasses high on his nose and tipping his head back to peer underneath. He was afraid of slipping on the sheets of ice that reflected the holiday lights like broken mirrors. "Do you think the murderer still has traces of poison on him?" he asked as they walked. The

late afternoon was so cold that every breath transformed into a small cloud of vapor.

"I doubt it, but if he thinks he's safe, he might have the bottle in a drawer or some other hiding place," Agatha hypothesized. "Strychnine is a fairly common substance, but in this case, it would be irrefutable proof of the crime."

Chandler nodded seriously. Then he heard a ringtone in his pocket and fished out a cell phone. "Miss Agatha, there's a call for you," he said.

Agatha's parents had bought her a cell phone, but since she preferred printed words to technology, Agatha often left it with the butler. She held the phone to her ear, which was numb with cold.

"Oh, it's you!" she exclaimed happily, then added, "Of course, yes . . . a tube of cobalt blue . . . okay, sure. We should be back in time for dinner!" She handed the phone back to Chandler.

"Was that my brother?" Dash sounded

surprised. "I didn't think he'd have a phone in that ramshackle studio of his . . ."

"Actually, he was calling from his neighbor's kitchen," she said with a laugh. "Do you see any art supply stores around here? In Montmartre, there was one on every corner. I should have remembered then!"

As they surveyed the shops, they spotted a glowing sign for the hotel Coeur Amoureux a few blocks from the Arc de Triomphe and immediately forgot about Gaston's request.

They sat on a bench to strategize. After a rapid exchange of ideas, they agreed that Agatha and Chandler would do the questioning, while Dash did his best not to get caught while searching for strychnine.

Dash was the first to step inside the hotel's plush lobby. It smelled of lavender and was decorated with white furniture, vases of flowers, lace curtains, and pink armchairs covered with

velvety cushions.

The boy stopped short on the heart-shaped rug in the lobby. "Uh, um, what's going on here?" he asked, confused.

"The Coeur Amoureux caters to honeymooners," replied Agatha, joining him. "What did you expect from a hotel called 'The Lovers' Heart' with a neon sign covered in flashing hearts?"

Chandler raised an eyebrow as though he disapproved of the glitzy atmosphere.

Agatha approached the front desk. The lady working at reception wore a candy-

pink dress and a necklace of violet pearls.

"*Bon soir, Madame.* We're looking for John Radcliffe and Marlene Dupont," Agatha said in her most charming voice.

"Are you friends of the bride and groom?" asked the lady with a big smile. She picked up the intercom. "Shall I let them know you've arrived?"

"Oh no, we'd like to surprise them," lied Agatha.

The lady pointed at the staircase and said, "Room two zero four, second floor."

"Thank goodness it's not the sixth for once!" Dash exclaimed.

Moments later they knocked on the door.

"Marlene, is that you?" called an anxious voice from inside. "Oh, my love, I knew you'd come back to me!"

They heard hasty footsteps, a key turning in the lock. A man in his thirties threw open the

door. He had dark blond hair and a crumpled but elegant suit. His face flooded with disappointment. "Who are you?" asked John Radcliffe, scratching his stubbly chin.

Agatha took the situation in hand. "We work for a private detective agency," she replied. "We'd like to ask you some questions, if you don't mind."

Radcliffe went pale and sat on the edge of the sofa, gripping the arm. "Did something terrible happen to Marlene?"

"It's not about Marlene," said Agatha. "May we step inside for a moment?"

He invited them in with a hasty nod.

During their last Metro trip, they had studied the couple's file. John Radcliffe was a brilliant New York attorney, while his pretty girlfriend, Marlene Dupont, lived on the outskirts of Paris, where she designed and sold hats. They had met six months earlier in Marlene's shop during one

of the charming lawyer's business trips to Paris.

"Is it about the murder on the Eiffel Tower?" he whispered. "TV stations all over the world are following the investigation."

Before Agatha could reply, Dash grabbed her attention, pointing repeatedly at the bedside table.

Leaning against a Cartier jewelry box was a single red rose, its long stem wrapped in gold foil.

It was identical to the one in the photo.

In a well-timed move, the butler positioned himself next to Radcliffe so Dash could observe the room with his special glasses.

"Mr. Radcliffe," Agatha began, "could you tell us what happened last night at the restaurant?"

The lawyer rubbed his forehead. "Everything was just perfect," he sighed. "Marlene had booked a table at the Jules Verne to celebrate my return to Paris. It was wonderful, better than ever. We were

gazing down at the city lights, holding hands. Unfortunately, after dinner I was so caught up in the romantic atmosphere that . . ."

Agatha eyed the Cartier box on the bedside table; it was just the right size for an engagement ring. "You asked her to marry you?" she queried.

He raised his head suddenly, his eyes shiny with tears. "It was the perfect occasion," he lamented, more and more upset. "I gave her a red rose as a token of my love, and she blushed and lowered her gaze. Then I presented the ring. Marlene went quiet and just stared around the

restaurant. She seemed overwrought. She told me that she wasn't ready for marriage . . . we had been together for such a short time. She got up and ran away in tears. She was so distraught that she bumped into a waiter and two other guests . . ."

"Do you remember what time it was?" Chandler interrupted.

"It was nine o'clock on the dot," replied Radcliffe with confidence. "I couldn't possibly forget it, because a split second later I was dazzled by the lights of the Eiffel Tower. You know, the ones that come on every hour with a big flash . . ."

Agatha had read a detailed description of the tower's famous lights. She nodded, stroking her nose. John's story seemed plausible, especially since he seemed so heartbroken. But she wanted to dig just a little more. "What did you do after Marlene ran out so abruptly?" she asked, pulling

out the blueprints to double-check the position of their table.

"I waited for a while, hoping that she might come back to my arms. Then I heard a shout over my shoulder and the room erupted in chaos. I was so upset that I barely noticed. I paid the bill and left in the private elevator."

"Can you think of anything else?" asked Agatha. "Did you notice anything unusual?"

He thought for a moment. "An ambulance with sirens blaring arrived at the front of the tower . . ." He shook his head. "That's all. Do you have any news about my sweet Marlene? I've been calling her home phone and cell phone all day, but she doesn't pick up. I'm afraid I've lost her forever!"

Agatha wanted to comfort him and promised she'd let him know if they heard anything about his lost love. Then they thanked him and left. She didn't waste any time asking Dash if he'd

found any traces of poison in the hotel room; she already knew his response. "Another dead end," he sighed as they walked out of the Coeur Amoureux. The lilac lights of the sign flashed shadowy hearts on his coat.

"There's still one red rose left, Miss Agatha," Chandler tried to console her. "We'd better hurry."

Strangely, Dash didn't seem worried about their stalled investigation. He hunched over, rubbing his belly.

"What's up, cousin?" Agatha asked him, concerned.

He clenched his teeth. "Hunger pangs. I skipped breakfast and lunch . . . I've had nothing but Coke all day long," he moaned. "Could we pick up some fast food?"

It was almost seven o'clock, and Agatha felt the urge to make one final effort. "Come on, I'm sure we're just minutes away from solving the

crime," she said in encouragement. "The third red rose lives just a few blocks away, on the Rue de Tintin!"

Dash adjusted his glasses. "You're right, duty calls!" he cried, straightening up. He didn't realize that "a few blocks" in an old city like Paris could become an exhausting maze.

Criminal Canapés

It was eight o'clock, and the lights of Paris were dimmed by the swirling snow. The only point of reference was the brightly lit forged-iron tower rising up above the rooftops, its shape so familiar from postcards and souvenirs that it barely seemed real. A thousand-foot tower, designed by the visionary engineer Gustave Eiffel for the 1889 World's Fair, which welcomed millions of tourists every year.

These tourists, however, did not include Agatha, Dash, and Chandler. They were trying to investigate a murder that took place in its second-floor restaurant without being able to

set foot in the tower itself.

That fact could potentially compromise their mission.

Dash dragged his feet as though he had invisible chains around both ankles. "Are we at the Rue de Tintin yet?" the Eye International student whined every time they reached a corner.

After his hundredth complaint, his cousin pronounced the magic words: "Yes, Dash, this is the Rue de Tintin."

Finally, some good news!

During their long slog through the snow, Dash had listened as Agatha and Chandler discussed the final red rose, Roxanne Pigafette. She was in her sixties, unmarried, and worked as a food critic for the *Michelin Guide,* the most important gastronomical guide in the world.

That particular detail made Dash's mouth water. Surely such a gourmet would know how to cook, and given the hour, perhaps she was

already cooking up something delicious . . .

The next news was far less hopeful. "The eighth floor?" he cried in desperation when they reached the right building. "I'll never make it!"

"There's no need to take the stairs this time," Agatha reassured him, pointing at the petite elevator. "Get your glasses programmed. Madame Pigafette is preparing canapés, and she said over the intercom that she doesn't have much time for us!"

At the word *canapés*, Dash vaulted into the elevator and pressed the button to close the door. Chandler managed to stick his foot inside just before the rest of the group was left behind.

"Forget anyone?" he asked quietly.

"Uh, oh, sorry about that," said Dash. "I'm just starving!"

They rode up, squished one against the other, holding their breaths with anticipation. As they walked down the marble-tiled hall on the top

floor, they spotted Madame Pigafette standing at the doorway of her luxurious apartment. She wore the same dress she'd had on the evening before: a black velvet sheath embroidered with red roses.

Was this where their investigation would end?

Was she the murderer of Boris Renko?

To find out, they would need to use every trick of the trade and follow Agatha's elaborate plan to perfection.

Her soft, wrinkled lips framed a greeting in English. "Good evening, my dears."

"Good evening, Madame Pigafette," replied Agatha.

Madame Pigafette hid a giggle behind her bony hand. "Please call me Roxanne," she declared. "*Madame* sounds too old."

Chandler gave a polite bow, tipping his cap, a gesture that caused a red flush to warm the food critic's pale face.

Pleasantries finished, she led the three Londoners into her parlor. The room had the feel of another era, furnished in walnut and rich burgundy velvet.

Platters of triangular sandwiches, a bowl of colorful dip, and a bottle of fine champagne were arranged on a low table.

Dash was ravenous. But just as he lunged for the food, he was stopped by a nudge to the ribs. "Do wash your hands first, dear cousin," said Agatha in a friendly voice. "We've been on the Metro, after all."

Remembering his role, Dash sprang up from the couch. "Uh, oh, excuse me Madame . . . I mean, um, Roxanne," he stammered, running his hands through his hair. "Where can I wash up?"

As soon as he left for the bathroom, Madame Pigafette dropped her voice, whispering to Chandler, "Detective, what a peculiar apprentice

you have. Why on earth is he wearing dark glasses at night?"

The butler was caught off guard, but quickly invented a lie that Dash suffered from a rare form of chronic conjunctivitis.

"Oh, the poor dear!" the old woman said sympathetically. "But back to us. What would you like to know about the terrible tragedy at the Jules Verne?"

Agatha got straight to the point. "Are you aware of the impact an incident like last night's homicide can have on a restaurant's rating?" she asked.

Madame Pigafette stared back at Agatha in bewilderment, not understanding her point.

"What I'm asking is this," the girl continued calmly. "After this tragedy, will the Jules Verne lose stars in the *Michelin Guide*?"

This was the factor on which the three investigators had based their suspicions.

Roxanne Pigafette's brother ran an elegant restaurant in the center of Paris, and was in constant competition with the Jules Verne. This famous food critic had an excellent motive to commit murder!

Until that point, their suspect had behaved with utmost courtesy, but Agatha's question infuriated her. "What are you implying?" she shrieked. "Do you think I killed that Russian diplomat to help my brother's restaurant?"

Her fiery reaction embarrassed Chandler, who reached for a sandwich.

"Stop!" Dash yelled from the doorway. "It's laced with strychnine!"

Everybody turned toward him and immediately saw the bottle of poison he held in his hand.

"B-but . . . what is that?" Madame Pigafette asked in surprise.

Dash approached the group with long

strides. "There are traces of strychnine scattered all across the kitchen floor, and I found this in the cupboard," he announced. "I bet it's the very same poison she used to dispatch Boris Renko!"

"Impossible, Dash," Agatha interrupted, shaking her head in disappointment. "Can't you see the label? It's a cockroach poison. All that would do is give someone a stomachache!"

"My apartment's infested with those horrid creatures," confessed an embarrassed Madame Pigafette. "They come out of the drainpipes and

run across my precious velvet. What else could I do?"

Like a dog with a bone, Dash insisted, "I'm sure you're very accomplished when it comes to lethal substances. You were even about to poison us!" He pointed dramatically at the platter of sandwiches, but his voice caught in his throat when he realized that his glasses weren't revealing so much as a trace of strychnine in the dishes on the table. Disappointed, he collapsed onto the sofa, while Agatha and Chandler did their best to apologize.

It was several minutes before they were able to calm the situation enough to continue their interrogation.

"Last night," Madame Pigafette began to recount, "I arrived at the restaurant just after nine p.m. I left my coat in the cloakroom and went to the ladies' room to freshen up. I had barely sat down at my table when an awful commotion

broke out and the restaurant emptied, except for the staff, a most disagreeable man with a camera, and a few curious onlookers. I left as soon as I could, without even ordering an aperitif."

"In the short time you were in the restaurant," asked Chandler, "did you notice anything strange?"

She paused to think, squinting her eyes. "The only thing that seemed out of place was the young woman holding the bathroom door open and peering out. I remember because when all the pandemonium broke out and everyone fled from the scene, she rushed toward the man who'd collapsed."

"A young woman?" repeated Agatha, her ears pricking up. "Can you describe her?"

Madame Pigafette shook her head. "I don't have a good memory for faces," she admitted. "But she didn't seem like a tourist. She looked like a chic Parisian dressed up for a date."

Agatha drummed the end of her nose with one finger. "Chandler, would you please show her the photo of Marlene Dupont?" she asked.

The butler had stashed the photo in a pocket in the cat carrier, and had to fight off a lively Watson to retrieve it. Even Dash, who was wolfing down sandwiches, stretched his neck in curiosity.

"That's her," the old woman confirmed once the photo was in her hands. "No doubt about it."

Exchanging triumphant looks, the three Londoners pulled on their coats in a hurry.

Roxanne Pigafette was confused by their sudden haste. "Would somebody please explain what's going on?"

"Your testimony pointed the way to the culprit," explained Agatha, running to the door. "Thank you so much, Madame. And bon appétit!"

As they rode back down in the elevator, Agatha asked Dash to check another Parisian

address on the EyeNet Plus GPS. "It all ties up with a bow!" she exclaimed. "Marlene's hat shop is on Lannes Boulevard—right across from the Russian embassy!"

$\mathcal{D}$ash nearly jumped out of his skin with excitement as they rode on the near-empty Metro. "Can you fill me in one more time?" he asked Agatha. "I think I missed a few steps along the way."

Chandler raised an eyebrow. "As did I, Miss Agatha."

The girl leaned one elbow against the window, counting off the evidence with her free hand. "Let's start with the first red flag," she began. "Madame Pigafette recognized Marlene Dupont, but according to Marlene's boyfriend, Marlene had already left of the Jules

Verne in tears at that point."

Dash was picking bits of green *pistou* sauce from between his teeth. "Go on, we're all ears," he prompted.

Agatha stood, tapping her index finger against her lip. "Do you remember what John Radcliffe said about Marlene's behavior just before her hasty exit?"

"Not in so many words," replied Chandler. "Could you please remind us?"

"He said Marlene was quiet and kept looking around the room anxiously. He thought she was upset by his marriage proposal, but suppose there was another motive: From her position in the restaurant, she would have been able to track Boris Renko's every movement!"

Dash verified the positions of the relevant tables on the EyeNet Plus. "You always manage to nail it," he noted. "But I don't understand why she'd be keeping an eye on a Russian diplomat."

"Because," reasoned Agatha, "she wanted to know which wine he had ordered from the sommelier, so she could put the poison in the right glass!"

Her two companions stared at her in amazement.

"Listen closely," she continued excitedly. "Do you know how a sommelier does his job in a fancy restaurant? The bottles of wine are kept in a separate area, and the sommelier brings wine to one table at a time." She gave Dash a meaningful look.

"I get what you're saying, but how did Marlene manage to put the poison into his glass?"

Agatha's gaze lit up. "We have to admit, she was quite ingenious," she continued. "Let's go back to John Radcliffe's story. He said that Marlene was so upset that she bumped into other guests as she left. Now, look carefully at the restaurant blueprints. To reach the exit—or the

ladies' room—Marlene would have had to pass next to the wine bar, which is where the glasses were, too . . ."

"She took advantage of the scene by distracting everyone, including the sommelier!" exclaimed Dash.

"And knowing which wine Mr. Renko had chosen, she slipped the strychnine into the glass that had been poured for him," concluded Chandler.

Agatha winked. "All clear, dear colleagues?"

They nodded, admiring her cleverness.

"But that's not the end of the story," Agatha went on. "We still don't know why, instead of just leaving the restaurant, Marlene hid in the bathroom and watched her plan unfold, while her boyfriend walked out with his tail between his legs. This makes me think that the whole thing was planned with utmost precision: the booking at the Jules Verne, the alibi she gave to John Radcliffe, who didn't even know he'd been tricked, and her knowledge of Mr. Renko's movements." She paused, lost in thought. "The only thing that escapes me for now is the motive for murder," she added, tapping her nose. "I'll need your help to figure that out."

"Wait," interrupted Dash. "Before we start examining possible motives, why are we going to Lannes Boulevard?"

"Because Marlene is hiding in her shop, obviously," his cousin explained. "Her boyfriend

didn't look for her there, for one simple reason: It's Sunday. The shop would be closed."

"And where does the Russian embassy come into all of this?" asked the butler, starting to sweat with the effort of keeping up with Agatha's lightning-fast reconstruction of events.

Agatha gave him a little smile. "Don't you think it's strange that a Russian diplomat was the victim, and Marlene's shop is right across from the Russian embassy? That's probably how she was able to keep an eye on him, study his daily habits, and pick the right moment to strike!"

"Then maybe her motive is related to some sort of espionage," he replied. "Maybe something that happened a long time ago."

"Excellent theory," Agatha complimented him. Then her eyes widened as an idea struck. "Can you repeat that last sentence, Chandler?"

"I said, maybe her motive goes back to something that happened in the world of

espionage a long time ago," repeated the butler.

Agatha let out a squeal of elation. "Dash, run a global search on the EyeNet for a spy called Marlene Dupont!"

Dash obeyed instantly. He knew they were nearing their destination, so he typed as fast as he could. "Nothing," he whispered bitterly.

"Do you think you could hack into the Russian embassy's database?"

"Normally I wouldn't be able to dream of it," he said with a grin. "But this is Agent UM60's EyeNet Plus, and it can work miracles."

He hunched over the device, concentrating hard. After a few attempts, he punched a victorious fist in the air. "I'm inside their archives, Agatha," he crowed. "What should I search for?"

"Try Marlene Dupont again."

"Nothing!"

Agatha realized there was only one stop left before they reached Lannes Boulevard. They

needed to come up with a new angle, but nothing came to mind. At the last minute, she proposed, "Try *red rose*!"

Dash threw himself into the search. The moments crept by as in a slow-motion film.

The doors opened as the loudspeaker advised them that they'd arrived at their stop. They hurried outside and were faced with a wall of white tiles. The station was empty and the cold was so intense that the hairs on the backs of their necks stood up.

"Well?" asked Agatha, on tenterhooks.

Even Chandler tried to peek at Dash's EyeNet.

"*Red rose* didn't bring up a thing!" said Dash in despair.

Agatha punched her fist into the palm of her other hand. "This is a huge problem," she observed. "If we can't find a link between Marlene and the victim, we'll never figure out her motive to murder him."

Chandler was dead silent. Dash scratched his head nervously. Agatha bit her fingernails.

"Unless . . ." she started.

The other two were hanging on every word.

"But of course!" Agatha exploded, her voice echoing through the empty station. "Mr. Renko's emergency call to Eye International was in English, but his native language is Russian!"

"So what?" asked Dash. "I don't see what you're getting at."

"It was a coded message for Agent UM60 to interpret!"

"I still don't get it," replied Dash.

"Red rose!" exclaimed Agatha. "Try

translating it on a Cyrillic keyboard."

He looked at her blankly.

"The Russian alphabet!" she said. "Try it!"

Dash lowered his head, clicking open an auto-translation program.

After a few moments, the screen flashed with two words in the Cyrillic alphabet;

красная роза

"What does *that* mean?" screeched Dash. "What are we supposed to do with some mysterious Russian words?"

"Master Dash, I suggest you run a search for it in the embassy's archives," Chandler offered. He had intuited his young mistress's line of thought. Meanwhile Agatha squeezed her eyes into two narrow slits, as though expecting a revelation at any moment.

And that is exactly what happened . . .

"Whoa!" exclaimed the young detective as he read the result of his search on the screen.

"Krasnaya Roza—Red Rose—was the code name of a famous spy who disappeared in the nineteen eighties under mysterious circumstances. His name was Sergei Ivanov, and he operated in Paris for decades during the Cold War. He even had a family here. Then he was fired by one of his superiors . . ."

"Boris Renko!" Agatha finished his sentence.

Dash stared at her, trembling. "Do you want to know the most amazing thing?"

"I already do, my dear cousin," she said, heading toward the street. "He was Marlene Ivanova Dupont's father!"

Terror on the Rooftops

The three detectives hurried along Lannes Boulevard at top speed. It was a busy street full of cars, with dazzlingly bright fog lights shining in their eyes.

Rushed as they were, they had to judge their steps carefully so they wouldn't slip on the slick, icy pavement. They were tired, and the cold seemed to seep into their bones.

It was 9:30 p.m., and they'd traveled the length and breadth of Paris, but they couldn't stop now—not when they were so close to bringing a murderer to justice.

"What's the plan?" asked Dash, out of breath.

"First we find Marlene, then we figure out how to catch her!" replied Agatha.

"I love it when we improvise," said Chandler. His sarcasm came as such a surprise that Dash and Agatha both burst out laughing, despite the snow and the bustling Parisian traffic.

Agatha signaled to her companions to stop. "I think we've already passed the hat shop," she panted. "It should be a lower street number." In the long day's excitement, even her cast-iron memory was beginning to lose its touch.

"How did we miss it?" asked Dash.

She pointed at the icy fog swirling around them. "It's just a minor setback; nothing to worry about," she reassured him. They retraced their steps, keeping close to the stores to better check every address.

"Here it is!" shouted Chandler.

Agatha motioned him to lower his voice and joined him in front of the closed roller shutter door.

"You're hiding inside there, I know it," she muttered through clenched teeth, as though there were a personal challenge between her and Marlene Dupont.

"What is our plan?" demanded Dash.

"We could knock and pretend we're police," suggested the butler. "Perhaps we'll be able to apprehend her without resistance."

Agatha shook her head and looked around, searching for a solution. After a quick reconnaissance, she observed, "The store has three entrances: the main one, a back door, and a grate that leads to a basement storage level. We'll go underground."

"Underground?" asked Dash.

"Didn't I tell you that there's a whole other world underneath Paris?" she joked.

"Well, yeah!" replied Dash. "But how will we get inside? Whichever door we choose, we'll need to break in!"

"Do you really think this is the time to worry about the law, Dash?"

Dash bristled. "I didn't mean that," he grumbled. "It's just that we'll need tools to cut chains, lift grates, or pick locks . . ."

Just then, Watson pushed through the door of his cat carrier, jumped down, and slipped through the iron grate near the sidewalk.

"Oh, no!" cried Agatha. "Watson, come back here!"

Calling him was useless—the cat had disappeared into the basement below the store.

"It looks like we'll have to go down there," said Agatha, looking around her. "But where's Chandler? Has he disappeared, too?"

The butler reappeared a moment later with a large steel bar in his hands. "I found this in one of the Dumpsters. I'll lift up the grate," he said, breathing hard. "Then I'll stand guard in front of the back entrance. Unfortunately, I'm

too big to slip through this opening . . ." he apologized.

Agatha thanked him for his initiative, and together they made a lever to lift the iron grate. After a great effort, they heard the *CLANG!* of bolts releasing.

"You're in, kids. Be careful!" said the butler.

He didn't need to say it twice.

With some difficulty, Dash eased himself through the narrow opening. When he reached the floor, he reached a hand up to his cousin to help her climb down.

They were in total darkness, except for the dim light sifting through the grate from the street above.

"What do we do now?" whispered Dash.

"We go upstairs to the shop and get Marlene to confess," replied Agatha softly.

"How about we turn on a light?"

"I'd rather we didn't announce our arrival,"

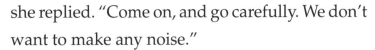

she replied. "Come on, and go carefully. We don't want to make any noise."

Just then, they heard the sound of something thumping around upstairs. It was probably Watson, who had apparently made his way into the hat shop.

"Ugh, what is this?" Dash hissed suddenly. He had bumped into a mannequin and was holding a plastic head in his hands. Agatha could tell he was trembling with fear, but she put her index finger to her lips.

They slowly made their way to the staircase and tiptoed up the stairs.

Behind them, a silent movement escaped their notice.

"Can you open the door?" asked Dash, his heart pounding.

Without a word, Agatha twisted the handle and crept forward stealthily. Silvery light slanted into the store from a small window. They saw shelves stacked with hats as they moved furtively toward the counter.

The tension was nearly unbearable.

"We've found you, Marlene!" announced Agatha in a steady voice. "We're private detectives! Come out from your hiding place!"

Dash heard footsteps behind him, and spun around just in time to drop to the floor, pulling Agatha down with him. A blond woman with a long, sharp hat pin missed them by a hair.

Marlene had followed them up from the basement, where she had watched them from her hiding place amid the mannequins. "You think

I'm trapped?" sneered the young murderess. "You'll never catch me!" She sped up a flight of spiral stairs in a corner of the store.

They tried valiantly to catch up with her, but quick as the wind, she climbed out onto the snow-covered roof. She paused behind the building's smoking chimney.

"Nosy snoops!" she said angrily. "I thought the intruder was my stupid boyfriend, but instead I find myself trailed by two amateurs playing detective."

Dash looked down at the sloping roof and grabbed hold of Agatha's sleeve. It was a thirty-foot drop to the street. If they were to slip, they wouldn't stand a chance. But Agatha continued to walk resolutely toward Marlene, and he was forced to swallow his fear and follow her.

"Why did you kill Boris Renko?" asked Agatha, a few paces away from the murderess.

"Revenge, you stupid little girl!" hissed Marlene with a nasty snicker. "Many years ago, that rat Renko betrayed my beloved father,

sending him on a one-way trip to Siberia. That's when I started to work on my plan for the perfect crime! The Jules Verne was the ideal place to avoid being discovered."

"But why did you stay in the restaurant after you poisoned him?" Agatha asked. "Why didn't you make a run for it?"

"I wanted that rat to recognize me," she replied darkly. "I went over to him and smiled in his face. I wanted him to remember what he had done to my family!"

At that moment, a flash of white zoomed between Agatha's and Dash's legs and launched itself at the murderess. It was Watson, more ferocious than ever, his jaws wide open and claws outstretched.

Marlene dodged him and started to laugh. "Even your little cat is going to meet the end it deserves," she snapped. As she began moving toward them, her face was suddenly lit up with

well-aimed red lights that soon striped the rest of her body.

They looked like little laser sights.

The reinforcements had arrived!

Marlene Dupont had no choice but to surrender. Men in the uniform of the French special forces emerged from behind the chimneys of the neighboring houses, surrounding her. In a matter of moments they arrested her and took her away in a helicopter that seemed to appear out of nowhere.

It happened so fast that Agatha and Dash just stood there with their mouths agape.

Who could have called the special forces?

The answer to that question came mere minutes later, when Agatha, Dash, and Chandler sat down to rest on the carpeted floor of the hat shop.

"Your phone is vibrating, Master Dash," the butler advised him.

Exhausted, with his heart still pounding, the young Londoner picked up a call from a number that he didn't recognize. "Who's this?"

"Excellent work, detective," Agent UM60 congratulated him. "You've fulfilled our agreement perfectly!"

Dash straightened up. "Oh, uh, is that you, professor? How are you doing? Where are you?" he stammered.

A video image of his teacher in a hospital bed, one leg in traction, appeared on the screen.

"I'm right here in London, but also in Paris." Agent UM60 gave a benevolent chuckle.

Agatha and Chandler craned over Dash's shoulders to see the small screen.

"I don't get it," said Dash. "London or Paris?"

"I told you, I'm in both places at once!"

Agatha pointed at the glasses with the LEDs. "Cousin, I think your professor has been observing all day through those glasses," she smiled. "And he's also been listening in on our conversation, am I right?"

"Excellent deduction, Miss Agatha," replied Agent UM60. "When I saw you were in a tight spot, I called the special forces to intervene."

Dash scratched his head. "So . . . um . . . you won't tell anybody at school that I caused your accident?" he murmured as Agatha lifted her eyebrows.

Agent UM60 grew serious. "The terms of our agreement were clear. If you succeeded with

this mission, you would not be expelled, Agent DM14," he stated. "I'll see you in class next week, by which time we will both have forgotten about that unfortunate incident, *oui*? Case closed."

The screen went black, and the lights on Dash's glasses turned off for the first time all day.

He leaped to his feet and started to jump up and down. Then he hugged his cousin and Chandler. "My detective career is saved!" he rejoiced.

Mystery Solved...

*T*he morning sun pierced the clouds and melted the snow. All of Paris sparkled like an enormous diamond.

Agatha, Chandler, and Dash had arranged to meet Gaston on the second level of the Eiffel Tower. They stood at the rail, gazing down at the city in all its splendor: its glorious buildings and well-tended gardens, the mazes of cobblestone streets, and the winding path of the River Seine.

It was three o'clock in the afternoon. They'd all slept late and eaten a delicious breakfast of fresh-baked croissants, so they were full of energy.

"You do realize that we only solved this case

because of pure luck?" Agatha said to Dash as they admired the view.

"Luck?" asked the young detective. "What do you mean?"

"I mean the red rose," said Agatha. "If John Radcliffe hadn't chosen a red rose for his marriage proposal, we would never have found our way to Marlene Dupont."

Dash thumped his chest proudly. "I'm sure we would have worked it out some other way," he declared. "We're an unbeatable investigative team, my dear cousin. Your brains and my expertise!"

She gave him a half smile and walked toward Chandler.

The butler was scrutinizing the city with a telescope, which looked like an ear of corn in his enormous hands.

"What time is Gaston supposed to arrive?" she asked him.

"He's already twenty minutes late, Miss Agatha," the Mistery House jack-of-all-trades replied calmly. "Maybe he's still adding finishing touches to the family portrait."

"He was so angry when he realized we'd forgotten to bring him that color he asked for," she recalled, laughing. "He's just like his brother!"

Chandler grinned. "While you were sleeping, I heard him grumbling at his easel about how it's not possible to paint a true work of art without cobalt blue."

"What did I tell you? He's a whiner, just like Dash!" Agatha laughed.

The tower was flooded by hordes of tourists pouring out of the elevators to take in the view. It was another half an hour before the young painter emerged from the stairwell.

"I came the whole way up on foot," he said breathlessly. "I didn't want to wait in that endless line for the elevators." He was clutching a frame

in his hands, covered by a drop cloth flecked with spots of dried paint.

The group gathered around a small bench.

"Ah, did you hear the news?" exclaimed Gaston, looking toward the Jules Verne restaurant behind them.

"What news?" asked the others.

"Didn't you hear about the murder on Saturday night?" asked the painter. "A Russian diplomat. They caught the culprit in record time."

"Did they really?" asked Agatha, feigning surprise.

"Forget about that," Dash said abruptly. "Let's see this great painting."

Dash was adamant about one point: No one, not even his brother, was allowed to know he attended a famous detective school. This was why they had been so vague about their activities the day before, and had not breathed a word to Gaston about their mission.

"*Oui*, I suppose crimes aren't exactly your sort of thing . . ." said Gaston, scratching his sideburns. "But I hope my *fantastique* work of art will arouse your interest!"

"Come on, what are you waiting for?" Dash encouraged him, relieved that he'd managed to change the subject.

"We can't wait to see it, Gaston!" Agatha added.

The painter wandered away into the crowd. "We need to find the perfect light," he explained, zigzagging from one side of the viewing platform to the other. "No, this won't do! Too much direct sunlight!"

In the end, he stopped in front of a warmly lit souvenir stand and leaned the frame against an iron bar.

The others had followed him through the crowd of tourists, and were ready to view the artwork Gaston had entitled *London Meets Paris.*

"Are you ready, *messieurs et mademoiselle*?" asked Gaston, one hand on the drop cloth.

They nodded. He whipped off the cloth, revealing the small group posed against the backdrop of a window that revealed the snow-covered Notre Dame cathedral. Agatha was writing intently in her notebook, Watson was curled up next to her, Chandler was punching a boxing-gloved fist in the air, and Dash posed with a pair of skis and his dark sunglasses.

The only problem was the sky in the view through the window behind them. It was the vivid lime-green of a lizard, or an energy drink.

"Wh-what's with that color, big brother?" asked Dash.

Gaston glowered at him, and answered resentfully. "That's what you get when there's no cobalt blue."

Agatha began to applaud and Chandler gave the young artist a pat on the back. Only Dash seemed dissatisfied, retreating behind his high-tech glasses. "That sky is so ugly that I'll need to activate the night-vision function just to avoid seeing it," he whispered to Agatha.

She turned to him, stunned. "Night vision? Why didn't you use that function last night when we were stumbling around in that basement trying to find Marlene?"

Dash covered his face with his hands. "I really am a bumbling detective," he whispered,

flushing with embarrassment. "I hope UM60 didn't think of it, either."

"Don't worry; you can make up for it on the next investigation," Agatha tried to console him. "Meanwhile, let's enjoy our first front-page newspaper story!"

Dash was speechless, but his expression changed when his cousin shoved a copy of *Le Figaro* under his nose. There was a photo of Marlene on the front page, along with a short article about the part played by two young British tourists in resolving the case.

"Naturally they couldn't print our names for security reasons," Agatha added quietly.

Dash was over the moon. "I'm famous!"

"What did you say?" interrupted Gaston. "Who's famous?"

Agatha smiled. "You are—or will be. He's talking about your extraordinary artwork," she said with a chuckle. "Why don't you paint a

whole series with Dash in different poses?"

Dash shot her a glare behind his brother's back.

"I'll get to work on it right away," Gaston declared solemnly. "Now that I've picked up an extra-large tube of the best cobalt blue."

Agatha

Girl of Mystery

Agatha's Next Mystery:
The Treasure of the
Bermuda Triangle

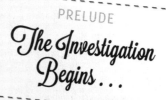

The Investigation Begins...

$\mathcal{I}$t was a blustery Saturday morning in late January, and Dashiell Mistery, an aspiring detective at the prestigious Eye International Detective Academy, was jumping out of his skin with excitement. He had just received an Evite from his friend Mallory, inviting him to her birthday party.

Dash was thrilled. He'd dragged himself out of bed to sit through an online seminar on Espionage and Counter-Espionage, and had been struggling to cover his yawns for two hours when Mallory's message popped up on his screen. He managed to keep his eyes open till noon, said a polite good-bye to Professor DM31, and immediately opened Mallory's invitation.

Her party would start at eight o'clock at Fashionista, an exclusive club in the center of London. The theme was the seventies, and guests were invited to "dress disco" in honor of that era's most popular music. The Evite was covered with vintage graphics of people wearing bell-bottom pants, multicolored shirts with pointed collars, suffocatingly tight vests, and platform shoes with chunky wedged heels.

Dash loved costumes and disguises, and he decided to pull out all the stops. He was starving, so he wolfed down a takeout container of fries that had been in the fridge for at least three days. Then he started rummaging through his closet—but all he could find were jeans, T-shirts, and a couple of sweaters and suits his mother had bought him for special occasions. Nothing that said "seventies disco." Not even close.

He opened several websites at once, trying to find the right look. After browsing for an hour or so, he streamed a video clip of John Travolta in the film *Saturday Night Fever*. The actor's movements were graceful and hypnotic, and his formfitting white suit would be just the thing for the party.

There was a vintage-clothing boutique a few blocks from Dash's penthouse apartment. He dug out the last of his weekly allowance and got into the elevator. After combing through every sale rack and trying on several outrageous outfits, he hurried back home with a large shopping bag. He took a quick shower and began getting dressed. By seven o'clock he was standing in front of the full-length mirror in his mother's room, checking the final details of his costume.

"No girl will be able to resist me tonight!" He smirked as he buttoned the vest of his three-piece suit. He emphasized his coolness by striking a pose, with one finger pointed at the ceiling and a hand on his hip, like John Travolta doing the Hustle. To his great surprise, he pulled off the dance moves quite well.

All Dash needed was a quick spritz of cologne, and he would be ready to dance up a storm. He grabbed hold of the bottle and pumped the squirter.

"Oww!" he shouted as the spray shot straight into his eye. "That burns like crazy!"

He ran into the bathroom to wash his face. The hot water made him cry out again. He rubbed his face harder, and let out a fresh scream of pain. Finally, after what seemed like an eternity of torment, he dabbed a cool washcloth over his face and managed to find some relief. Taking a deep breath, he opened his eye and looked at himself in the mirror. The eye looked like a fireball!

"I'm going to need a gallon of eye drops! Where

did mom put them?" the young detective cried out in despair. Half-blinded, he wandered through the apartment, bumping into furniture and slipping on piles of magazines and comic books. "Maybe it's in the first-aid kit . . ."

He opened a cupboard, digging through the emergency medical kit in a frenzy. It was stuffed full of bandages, gauze, and disinfectant, but there were no drops.

Meanwhile, his eyelid had gotten puffy and swollen. "I can't go to the party looking like this!" he moaned. "I have to do something!"

He paced back and forth for a few minutes. It was already well past eight o'clock. The party would be in full swing by now. Suddenly, he snapped his fingers. "I'm such an idiot!" he cried. "Why didn't I think of that sooner?"

He had come up with a solution, and even if it looked a little ridiculous, it was the best he could do in an emergency.

Twenty minutes later he strolled into the party, whistling as if nothing had happened. He'd used styling mousse to sculpt a tuft of hair over one side of his face so that none of his friends would notice the inflamed eye hiding beneath it.

After greeting everyone, Dash scooped up an armload of snacks and found a free chair in a dark corner. The other guests all were dancing under an enormous disco ball that sent sparkling bursts of colored light around the room, but he wasn't sure if his improvised hairdo would stay in place if he started dancing.

"Aren't you going to get on the dance floor?" Clark asked him, shaking his hips in time to the music. "That's where all the girls are!"

Dash crossed his legs, tossing some popcorn into his mouth. "I'm saving my energy," he said, adopting a sophisticated tone. "The best dance tunes always come at the end!"

Clark chuckled, swinging his hips as he

disappeared into the crowd. The disco beat set the dance floor on fire. After a fast-paced song, Mallory danced over and pulled Dash's hand. "This is my big night, Dash," she giggled. "And if you don't get up off that couch, you're going to break all the girls' hearts!"

Dash was about to reply with a sarcastic joke, but a couple of birthday well-wishers pulled Mallory to the middle of the room to cut a huge cake that had appeared out of nowhere.

In the middle of all the commotion, Dash tried to figure out his next move. *This looks like the perfect time to cut and run,* he said to himself. *I can use my incredible diversionary tactics to slip out while no one is watching!*

But as soon as he got to his feet, he felt a light tap on his shoulder. "Are you leaving already?" asked a girl's voice. "Don't you like to party?"

Dash turned quickly and stared open-mouthed at the girl who had stopped him from leaving. She was tall and willowy, with cascading blond curls and dazzling emerald eyes. She was a total fox, no doubt about it.

"I've been watching you all night long," she confessed with a nervous giggle. "I'm always intrigued by eccentric types. Great suit, by the way." She held out her hand. "Do you have a name? I'm Linda."

"Umm . . . well . . . I'm, um, Dash," he stammered, embarrassed.

"How dashing! Would you like to dance?" Linda suggested.

"Umm . . . sure . . . I guess . . ."

They started to wend their way onto the dance floor. Suddenly, Dash reached into his pocket, which was vibrating like mad, and pulled out an odd-looking phone. It was the state-of-the-art tech device given to every Eye International student to help them carry out top-secret missions around the world.

Code name: EyeNet.

Dash read the text and turned pale as a ghost. "Are you kidding me? Talk about timing!" he cried. "I need to call Agatha immediately!"

"Who's Agatha?" asked Linda, suspicious. "She's not your girlfriend, is she?"

Dash was so worked up that he didn't even answer her. "Could I please borrow your phone? My reception is awful!" he cried.

Naturally this wasn't true, but he didn't want his teachers to intercept a call on the EyeNet and find out how much help he got with his investigations.

A moment later, he was back in the chair, sending a text to his cousin Agatha while Linda waited for him on the dance floor. As soon as he finished, he gave back her phone, apologized for the unforeseen interruption, and took off at top speed for Gatwick Airport.

A dangerous mission had just begun. Destination: the Bermuda Triangle!